THE

BANDS OF EVIL

I

As Scrooey-Looey walked through the farmer's field he was approached by a horrid hag carrying a tray of bubble-mixture around her neck. Each bottle was labelled "Super whizzo bubble-mixture. The biggest bubbles in the world." "Good morning, Mr Scrooey-Looey," said the horrid hag politely.

"Morning, hag," replied the rabbit. "My goodness! You are in need of plastic surgery."

The horrid hag trembled with anger but ignoring the remark continued politely: "Would you like to buy some boys a present? The best bubble-mixture in the world. Three bottles for 1p."

Scrooey-Looey had never bought anyone a present but three bottles for 1p was a bargain. Without thinking he handed over 1p, grabbed the bottles and ran, muttering to himself, "I've really got a bargain!" As he ran back to The Old Vicarage, the horrid hag laughed and disappeared.

Scrooey-Looey found the boys in the garden. They ran to him. "Bubble-mixture!" "Thank you, Scrooey-Looey," they cried, as they unscrewed the lids, dipped in the sticks and blew huge bubbles. The bubbles went right over them and trapped inside they floated up into the sky.

Scrooey-Looey was so shocked at what he had done that without thinking he climbed the highest tree (though he was scared of heights) and jumped off on to the bubble containing Benjamin as it soared up from below. He hung on and shut his eyes. The bubbles floated above the trees. A strange wind blew and carried them away towards the ruined tower in the glade deep within the forest.

Boris the skull was floating above the tower, looking out towards the village. "I can see three bubbles. One has a furry thing on top." "A furry thing!" exclaimed Griselda. "What is it?"

"A rabbit!" hissed Boris. "It must be Scrooey-Looey." "I'm not eating him," murmured Griselda. "He's so rude and disagreeable he would give me belly-ache. I shall use him to make a pair of white gloves. The carrion crow can eat the rest."

Inside the bubbles the boys could see the ruined tower. Scrooey-Looey still had his eyes shut tight as the bubbles landed lightly on the ground at Griselda's feet. "Run, Scrooey-Looey," shouted Benjamin. The rabbit jumped and ran.

"Catch him, guards," commanded Griselda. But the dwarves were too slow. They tripped over each other's feet and landed in a heap. Scrooey-Looey disappeared into the forest and hid in the bushes.

Griselda raised her magic staff and burst the bubbles. The boys fell to the earth amidst slimy, disgusting bubble-mixture. "Seize them, guards. Put them in the fattening cages."

The boys kicked and fought but, after a struggle, the dwarves threw them in the cages. "Ah, that is better," said Griselda poking Benjamin with her magic staff through the bars of the cage. "They are very bony. They need fattening up. Get the fattening mixture."

The dwarves went to the cages. They were too strong for the boys, and though the boys put up a fight, it was not long before they were fed. The dwarves hobbled away moaning loudly "Spat the mixture up my nose", "Kicked my shin," "Bit my ear".

Griselda looked in her cookery book. "Now let me see. I took a recipe from the Daily Witch and popped it in here. Ah, here it is. Pot roast for boys. I shall need dragon's blood, mashed newt, wings of bat and wriggling worms. I don't suppose you've got them," she cried looking at the dwarves. "Got the lot." "Good. The boys have fattened nicely. Throw them in the pot."

"Oh no," murmured Scrooey-Looey from behind the bushes. "How can I save them?" He could think of nothing.

II

Julioso took Julius, Aliano Alexander, Benjio Benjamin. The boys were so fat they could not struggle. The dwarves swung the boys in the air. Then the dwarves did a strange thing. They never knew themselves whether it was because that morning they were especially dim or because deep down they wanted to save the boys. But when they swung the boys in the air they flung them in the magic cauldron not the cooking pot. With loud cries the boys disappeared.

When Griselda saw what the dwarves had done, she screamed and screamed and screamed. The noise was so great Boris floated to the top of the highest tree. The dwarves ran and hid. "Do not think that you can hide from me," bellowed Griselda. She raised her magic staff: Julioso shot out from behind a water tower which stood to one side of the ruined tower and landed at her feet. She raised her magic staff again: Aliano flew out of a window of an attic in the ruined tower and landed on top of Julioso. She raised her magic staff the third time: Benjio shot out of a pile of manure and landed on top of Julioso and Aliano.

The dwarves trembled before Griselda. She raised her magic staff, uttered an ancient spell and bands of crystal appeared around their necks and wrists; at the front of each band there was a grinning skull.

"Go to Ramion and recapture my supper. When you find a boy take a band off your wrist and put it round his neck. The band will expand to any size. Rub the skull at the front and then the boy will travel to me. Once you have returned the boys to my tender care, rub the skull at the front of the band around your necks and you will also return to me. Do not fail to recapture the boys and then return or I shall come and atomise your cringing bodies."

Atomise was too hard a word for the dwarves to understand, but they knew it could not be nice to be atomised. "No, mistress," they stammered as they felt the hard bands around their necks. "We will not fail." "Now go." So saying, Griselda kicked the dwarves into the magic cauldron: with cries they disappeared. Griselda went into the tower. As soon as she had gone Scrooey-Looey crept out from behind the bushes, jumped into the magic cauldron and disappeared.

The boys landed deep within a jungle. They had returned to their normal size and picking themselves up walked slowly between the trees. They were tired and did not know that Griselda's guards were only just behind.

They saw flowers in the shape of trumpets, bent down and picked them. Soon their arms were full of flowers. A gentle breeze blew and the trumpets began to play a merry tune. The boys danced and danced until exhausted they lay down on a bank beside a jungle stream and fell asleep, flowers strewn all around.

The dwarves landed deep within the jungle, one on top of another. It took a long time to untangle muddled arms and legs. At last they got up, looked around and found a print from Benjamin's shoe. "The boys have been here. We must track them down."

When Scrooey-Looey landed, he gave a scream of delight: he was in a forest of lettuces and carrots fifty foot high. "Great! Great! Great! More! More! More!" he shouted as he began to eat.

Scrooey-Looey forgot all about the boys and the need to warn them that the guards were about to hunt them down. He ate and ate. He did not see the hairy caterpillar twenty foot long, two foot wide and high, until its jaws began to close around his head. Then he began to run.

The dwarves found the boys asleep on the bank beside the jungle stream, flowers growing all around.

"The flowers are beautiful," sighed Julioso.

"The boys are beautiful as well," sighed Aliano and Benjio.

The boys awoke, the sound of trumpets still dancing in their minds. They were not afraid of the dwarves. They scrambled to their feet and gave each dwarf a flower.

III

At that moment Scrooey-Looey arrived. "Give me one of your bracelets Julioso," said Scrooey-Looey. Hardly knowing what he did, Julioso slipped a bracelet off his wrist and handed it to Scrooey-Looey.

The caterpillar was just behind the rabbit. He was panting loudly for he was fat and out of breath. "I only wanted to play," he complained.

"Let's play Kings and Princes," said Scrooey-Looey, "You will be King and I will bow before you, but if you are King you must wear this special bracelet round your neck."

"What is that funny thing on the front of the bracelet?" asked the caterpillar. "Your family crest," replied Scrooey-Looey. "You come from a long line of noble caterpillars: your family crest is a human skull."

"Fancy that," said the caterpillar, not noticing that all the collars and bracelets worn by the dwarves bore a human skull. "Put it round my neck. Then bow down before me."

The bracelet expanded until it fitted round the neck of the caterpillar; Scrooey-Looey lightly rubbed the skull and with a grunt the caterpillar disappeared.

At that moment a tiger arrived looking for his supper. The dwarves screamed and huddled together in a heap. Scrooey-Looey (who had grown strangely brave) said to Aliano, "Give me one of your bracelets". Hardly knowing what he did, Aliano slipped a bracelet off his wrist and handed it to Scrooey-Looey.

"Great and mighty tiger," said Scrooey-Looey. "Before you do us the honour of eating us, may I give you this bracelet: a token of our high regard for your noble person."

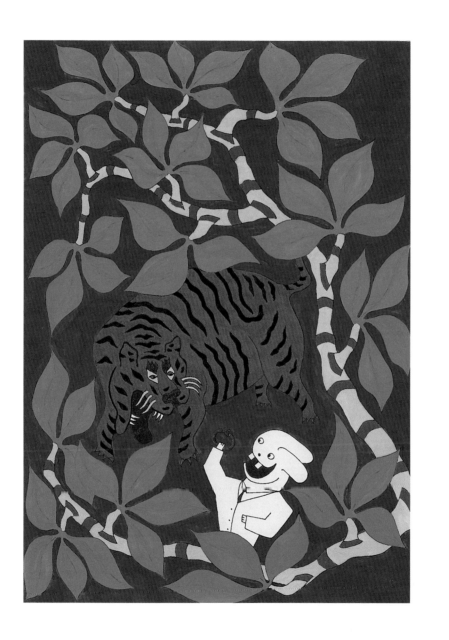

"For my noble person," said the tiger, much charmed by the speech. "It pleases my noble majesty to accept your gift. Then I shall do you the great honour of eating you for supper. Do I wear the bracelet on my paw?"

"No, your great and wondrous majesty," said Scrooey-Looey. "It expands like this. It would look most regal round your neck." Scrooey-Looey placed the bracelet round the neck of the tiger. The tiger looked at his reflection in the stream, as Scrooey-Looey lightly rubbed the skull and with a roar the tiger disappeared.

At that moment four cannibals arrived holding spears and shields. They were also looking for their supper. The dwarves screamed in terror as Scrooey-Looey said to them, "Give me your bracelets." Hardly knowing what they did, the dwarves slipped the bracelets off their wrists. They handed them to Scrooey-Looey.

"Great and noble warriors," said Scrooey-Looey. "Before you do us the honour of eating us, may I give you these bracelets: tokens of our high regard for your noble persons." The cannibals bowed: how nice to meet someone who knew how to behave before he was eaten.

"But what is that funny thing on the front of the bracelets?" asked the cannibals. "The skull of a missionary. Symbol of your mighty race." Much pleased, the cannibals bowed their heads as Scrooey-Looey placed a bracelet round each neck and Scrooey-Looey said: "The bracelets have a magic charm if you rub the missionary's head." Each cannibal raised an arm and rubbed the skull, and with loud cries disappeared.

"You are a marvel, Scrooey-Looey," said the boys, extremely pleased. But not the dwarves. They had just realised what they had done. Now that all six bracelets had been used they could not return the boys to Griselda. What was worse they had sent her a caterpillar twenty foot long, two foot high and wide, a tiger and four cannibals: she was not likely to be pleased. "She will hunt us down and atomise our cringing bodies," groaned the dwarves as they ran deep into the jungle.

IV

"Ah Boris, Boris," murmured Griselda tickling the skull under the chin. "I think this time the guards will get those boys." "They are extremely dim." "But with the collars they will not dare to fail. They know that I will track them down and atomise their cringing bodies." "Fear will not give them brains."

"Boris, sometimes I think you are too brainy just to be a skull," murmured Griselda gloomily. "I hate it when you're right. Those dwarves have yet to catch a thing. They are bound to fail." She rose to her feet, muttering beneath her breath: "Hate it, hate it, hate it when you're right," and kicked Boris to the top of a tree (where he yawned, stuffed cotton wool in his ears and fell asleep). Leaving her magic staff beside the cauldron she wandered through the nettles and brambles murmuring, "I wish I had some guards with brains."

As Griselda walked, deep in gloomy thoughts, out of thin air appeared the caterpillar twenty foot long, two foot wide and high. It nearly landed on her head. "Boris! Boris!" shrieked Griselda. "Come to my aid." But Boris had cotton wool in his ears and was asleep at the top of the tree as Griselda ran round the tower pursued by the caterpillar.

Then out of thin air appeared the tiger. It nearly landed on her head. "Boris!! Boris!!" screamed Griselda. But Boris was still asleep as Griselda ran and ran pursued by the caterpillar and the tiger.

Then out of thin air appeared the four cannibals holding spears and shields. They nearly landed on her head. "Boris!!! Boris!!!" yelled Griselda, running round and round the tower pursued by the caterpillar, tiger and four cannibals. Although she was ugly and scrawny, they were very keen to eat her.

Boris awoke and looking out of the sockets where once were eyes saw his mistress panting, running round and round the tower pursued by the caterpillar, the tiger and four cannibals. Boris was strangely fond of Griselda. Deciding that he must help her, he floated down from the tree and with a beam from his eye sockets lifted up the magic staff and sent it flying into Griselda's outstretched hand. Griselda turned and raised the magic staff, uttered a curse and the caterpillar (who was just about to eat her) exploded in her face, covering her with juicy innards. "Yuk!" she cried. "That was a mistake. I had better turn the tiger into stone." She raised the magic staff, uttered a curse and the tiger (who was leaping on her) turned to stone. It pinned her to the ground. "That was a mistake," groaned Griselda. "Boris! Boris! Help!!! I cannot raise the staff. The cannibals will eat me."

The cannibals got out their knives and forks. They flavoured Griselda with salt and pepper and were just about to eat her when Boris turned his sockets on the water tower. Laser beams shone from the sockets, cut through a wooden pillar and the water tower crashed to the ground, sending a great wave flowing over Griselda and the four cannibals. It swept the cannibals away but not Griselda, for she was pinned to the ground by the stone tiger.

"Boris!" spluttered Griselda, wringing wet. "You stupid skull! I nearly drowned. Get this tiger off me."

Boris floated to his mistress and sent a beam from his eye sockets which blasted the tiger to smithereens, covering Griselda with pieces of stone and choking powder. "Boris!" she gasped. "There are times you are lucky that I cannot eat you." She was raging mad. "The caterpillar, tiger and four cannibals wore around their necks the bracelets which I gave the dwarves. Boris those useless dwarves have failed. I shall go and get those boys and atomise those dwarves."

Griselda blew her hunting horn, shouted, "Tally ho! Off we go!" kicked Boris into the magic cauldron and jumped in after him. With a cry they disappeared, landing in the jungle not far from the boys and Scrooey-Looey. "I smell boys," she cried with an evil laugh. She began to run. Boris floated on her shoulder.

V

"We must hurry," cried Julius, "before Griselda gets us." They ran and ran. Griselda was only just behind. "I'm tired out," cried Benjamin, "I can't run any further." "You must," replied his brothers, taking him by the hand as they ran and ran.

Then a lion jumped out in front of them. "Help! We're going to be eaten." "No, you're not," softly roared the lion. It was the lion of icing from Alexander's birthday cake. "But you disappeared in the rain!" exclaimed the boys. "I always do, but when the sun comes out I spring to life again."

The boys and Scrooey-Looey jumped up on the lion's back. The lion ran and ran towards the Garden. As he left Griselda far behind the flowers in the shape of trumpets played a joyful tune.

The sound of trumpets filled the forest, buzzing in Griselda's ears, mocking all her evil plans. Griselda groaned, cursed and ground her teeth in pain. As the smell of boys grew fainter she bellowed in anger, "The boys are escaping but I shall get those dwarves. I feel the evil from the bands around their necks. They cannot escape. I shall atomise their cringing bodies."

"She's going to get us," moaned Julioso as the dwarves ran. "Atomise our bodies," groaned Aliano. "Blast us into nothingness," added Benjio.

The bands around their necks grew heavier. "I can hardly breathe," gasped Julioso. "Griselda must be very near," sighed Aliano. "Let's hide in the bog," suggested Benjio, who was very dim.

The dwarves jumped into the bog and hid in the mud with just their noses showing.

Griselda arrived with Boris floating on her shoulder. When she saw the three noses sticking out of the mud, she laughed an evil sneering laugh: "You cannot escape from me." She pointed her magic staff at the bog and the dwarves rose up into the air, covering Griselda with mud and slime. They landed at her feet. "Yuk!" she screamed. "You've had it. This time you've really had it. I'm going to atomise your cringing bodies." The dwarves quaked with fear. They kissed her feet. They stammered, "No, mistress," "No", "No, please." "No good!" screamed Griselda as she raised her magic staff.

At that moment Boris whispered in Griselda's ear, "Who is going to fetch the rhino sick from the shop? Who is going to get the maggots, wriggling worms and wings of bat?" Griselda went pale, paused (servants are so very hard to get) and screamed at the skull, "Boris! I hate it when you're right." She kicked the skull as far as she could and trudged off into the forest.